For Rosemary Stimola, a lovely book hugger.
B.S.

For my beloved children: Mattéo, Salomé, and Joachim.
F.B.

Phaidon Press Limited
Regent's Wharf
All Saints Street
London N1 9PA

Phaidon Press Inc.
65 Bleecker Street
New York, NY 10012

phaidon.com

First published 2016
© 2016 Phaidon Press Limited
Text copyright © Barney Saltzberg
Illustration copyright © Fred Benaglia

Artwork created with ink on paper and painted digitally.
Typeset in Didot.

ISBN 978 0 7148 7284 1
001-0816

Designed by Meagan Bennett

Printed in China

Hug This Book!

by Barney Saltzberg

illustrated by Fred Benaglia

You can read this book to a hippo.

You can read this book in the bath.

If you read this book being tickled,
I dare you not to laugh!

You can kiss
and hug
and smell
this book.

That might sound
sort of silly.

You can wrap this book in a sweater,
if it ever gets too chilly.

You can make up a story
to tell to this book.

Or read it upside down.

You can read this book up in the air,
to
everyone
in
town.

Can you read this book
in the mirror?

Or sing the words in this book like a song?

If you sing it to the birdies,
maybe they'll sing along.

You can take a quiet nap with this book.

Maybe you'll hear it snore.

When you wake up,
find a grown-up,
and read this book some more.

You can spin
and twirl
and dance with this book.

You can listen while someone else reads it.

You can take your
book to lunch.

Just do not try to feed it.

Even though this book is over,
it isn't really the end.

You can start at the beginning
and read it to a friend!